Madame Cadillac's Ghost

A GREAT LAKES ADVENTURE
IN HISTORY & MYSTERY

To "Mrs. Beesley's B's"
Readers make leaders!
J.L. Panagopoulos
03/09/03

by

Janie Lynn Panagopoulos

D1622828

River Road Publications, Inc.
Spring Lake, Michigan

Jacket and book illustrations are by Don Ellens
The Panagopoulos drawing is by Carolyn Stich
Book design is by Patricia Westfield

ISBN: 0-938682-67-9

Dedicated to my friends and paddling pals,
the "Project Lakewell" guys:
Mark Chambers, Mike George, Mike Judd,
Kenn Kuester, Jim Ledford, Jim Meyerle,
Dave Whitaker, and Jean (Frenchy) Yargeau.

"May the water always be smooth
and the wind fair, and may
we always be ready for adventure."
–Janie

Contents

To the Reader...

Over 300 years have passed since Cadillac and his family first penetrated the North American wilderness to help settle the city that is known as Detroit, in Michigan's southeast corner. The city of Detroit is the remnant of an expedition of French men and women who dreamed of founding an empire that would cross the continent and make them wealthy.

Madame Cadillac's Ghost is a whimsical ghost tale created to help bring forth historical facts concerning the founding of the city of Detroit, its Native American history and traditional oral stories, and to remind the reader that our forefathers and -mothers suffered great hardships, dangers, and emotional strife that often led to superstitious imaginings and fearful anxiety.

The weaving of this tale, set in the Detroit Historical Museum, is based on the historical study and interpretation of original documents that serve as a framework for this book.

When you live with wolves
you learn to howl.

Antoine de la Mothe Cadillac

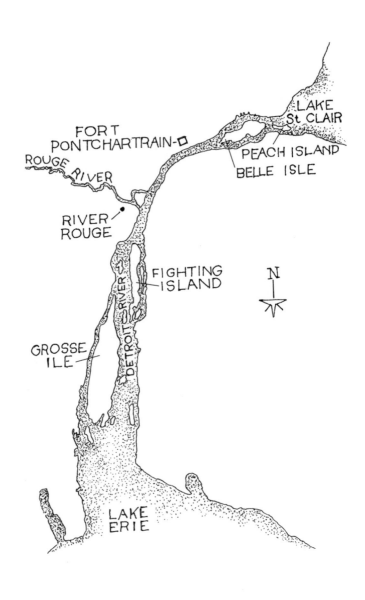

ROUGE RIVER

FORT PONTCHARTRAIN-

RIVER ROUGE

FIGHTING ISLAND

GROSSE ILE

DETROIT RIVER

LAKE St CLAIR

PEACH ISLAND

BELLE ISLE

N

LAKE ERIE

1

Belle Isle

"How much longer do we have to be in this little car?" whined Allie as her father sped along the roadway of **Belle Isle**.

"Allie, can't you just enjoy the ride?" he asked. "Look out the window at the **Detroit River**. This is the doorway to the Great Lakes. Just imagine, it was once an Iroquois warpath. The Iroquois came right through here when they invaded out of New York. The Iroquois called this area Tjeughsahrondie, but don't ask me what it means." He laughed and gazed back at his daughter in the rear view mirror.

"Detroit is incredible; it has a wonderful history. Just use your imagination. It's all still out there.

"In the early 1700s," he continued, "over 6,000 Native Americans lived in this area when the French **commandant** Cadillac was here. He built the first permanent French outpost, **Fort Pontchartrain**, to protect the **fur trade**. The **strait**—*le Détroit*—linked Swege, or what we call today Lake Erie, to the Great Fish Lake, or Lake Huron. This strait was the key to the upper-country trade for those that lived north and south of this point. It was the most important gateway of the time. *Le Détroit*, or Detroit as we call it now, means 'the straits.' That's how this place got its name."

Allie shook her head and looked out the window, wishing her father could talk without sounding like a history book. She watched as the river and trees quickly blurred by.

"Allie, don't be such a jerk. This is cool," Shoo blurted out in defense of his father.

"Is this really a race track, Dad? Do you think our van could go this fast on these curves?"

"You are not supposed to be driving so fast," said Mrs. Spywell sharply. "You're supposed to follow the speed limit, and no, Shoo, today this isn't a racetrack, it's a roadway."

"I'm driving the speed limit, dear, don't worry. But this is fun, driving where the **Detroit Grand Prix** is held." Allie's father sped around another curve that circled the tiny island in the straits of Detroit.

Allie's stomach began to churn and feel queasy as their car darted from lane to lane. Shoo, trying to bug his sister, swayed back and forth with each curve, and leaned hard against Allie's shoulder.

"Get over on your own side!" she snapped.

"Hey, I can't help it. Dad's car is small!"

said Shoo with a mean grin directed at his sister.

"Mom? When will the van be out of the shop? Dad's car is too small for the four of us, especially with Shoo."

"Enough!" demanded their mother. "Shoo, stay on your own side of the car and leave Allie alone. Do you understand?"

Shoo nodded his head as his mother peered at him over the car seat. When Mrs. Spywell turned around to face forward, Allie smiled at her brother and scrunched up her face. Shoo stuck out his tongue and put his fingers in his ears wiggling them at her, just as he caught a glimpse of his father watching him in the rearview mirror. Mr. Spywell cleared his throat and softly shook his head to Shoo, so as not to attract the attention of his wife.

Watching out the backseat windows, Allie and Shoo tried to focus on the rows of trees that lined the roadway and waterway. The skyline of Detroit looked like a gray-blue blob hovering over the river's edge. It sure is a big city, Allie thought.

As Allie tried to see out Shoo's window she noticed he was now holding tightly onto his seat belt shoulder strap, trying not to sway in her direction. The more Allie watched out the windows, the more her stomach rumbled.

"Oh, Dad, can we stop? I feel carsick," complained Allie.

"When we get around near Scott's fountain, why don't we pull over?" suggested her mother. "Allie can get some air and I want them to see the fountain, anyway. It's just about the only thing, except for the big trees, that I remember on the island from when I was a child. Besides, I would like to see something besides a blur while we're here," she commented to her husband with a grin.

"All right, all right, you win," said Mr. Spywell as he slowed the car down. "You know, if I hadn't became an archaeologist, I might have been a good race car driver. I always thought it would have been neat racing fast cars around and around a track. Just the smell of gasoline and rubber tires burning and the noise. Wouldn't that be great?"

"No thank you!" exclaimed Mrs. Spywell.

"I think being a race car driver would be real cool, Dad," interrupted Shoo. "If I don't become a **cryptozoologist** and discover the first Bigfoot in America, maybe I'll become a race car driver."

"A cryptozoologist?" Allie blurted out. "You will be lucky if you make it to middle school."

"Hey, what's that supposed to mean? I get good grades." Shoo reached over and nudged his sister on the arm. "I've been Student of the Month lots of times."

"What that means is you better leave me alone," snapped Allie. "Because I feel sick, and this car is really small." She glared at her brother who noticed she did look slightly green.

"All right, you two. The fountain is coming up. I'm stopping. I'm stopping!" said their father, interrupting their fight.

"Look to your right, Allie, there's Canada," said Mrs. Spywell trying to get Allie's mind off her stomach and to stop the argument with Shoo. As the car made the curve around the southern tip of Belle Isle, the Windsor, Ontario, skyline appeared to their right. In a flash, a large red car pulled up close beside them in the outside lane and rode there, blocking their view.

"Hey, get out of the way! I want to see Canada," growled Allie. "Geeze, just when

I thought I was going to see something."

"Wow, that car sure is red," said Shoo.

"It is bright," added their mother. "It almost looks like the color of lipstick."

"It's a Cadillac," said Mr. Spywell. "A real American product. Actually, a real Detroit product. You can't get better than that.

"Did you know **Henry Leland**, the man that created the Cadillac, worked with **Henry Ford** for a while and then finally sold his ideas to **General Motors**. Some say Henry Leland was the man that helped to create the auto industry with the Cadillac."

Allie rolled her eyes, "Dad, it's just a red car. . .who cares?" She gazed out over the hood of the intruding car, trying to get a glimpse of Canada, but it was no use. "I wish that Cadillac would just go away or speed up or something." Allie tried to concentrate, but her stomach kept reminding her of the two hot dogs, jumbo French fries, and double chocolate shake she had for lunch.

As the two cars drove side-by-side, Allie began to feel dizzy and her mouth tasted strange. I wish I could burp, she thought. Maybe I'd feel better.

"Dad! When are we going to stop? I'm really getting carsick," she whined and held her belly.

Shoo, ignoring his sister's complaint, laughed aloud. "Cadillac, wow, that's really funny. Isn't that the name of that French guy you were just talking about? That's weird. I wonder why anyone would name their kid after a car?"

Allie listened with her hands holding her stomach. Could her brother really be that dumb? Maybe it's him that's making me sick, she thought.

"Shoo, don't be silly. Cadillac wasn't named after a car. The car was named after him," corrected their mother as she cast a glance at her son over the car seat and shook her head. "Detroit is the **Automobile Capital of the World**. Didn't you know that? You know, **Motown**, Motor City."

"Duh," Allie squeezed out as she held her stomach and shook her head in disgust.

"Well, excuse me!" snapped Shoo as he scrunched up his shoulders.

"Dad, where's the fountain? Can you slow up or something so this car will pass? I'm really going to hurl."

"Oh, poor Allie," teased Shoo. "That double thick chocolate shake doing twists in your stomach with the French fries?"

"You want to see?" asked Allie in a cocky voice as she opened her mouth wide in her brother's direction. "Or maybe it's just you that's making me sick."

"All right, you two, stop it right now. Your father and I take you on these trips so you can see and learn something, and if all you're going to do is argue, we can go home right now."

"No. I just want to stop. I feel sick," whined Allie.

"And I want to go to the Detroit Historical Museum," added their father. "They have a great Motor City exhibit. Maybe they even have an old Cadillac there, or at least some pictures. So you both better straighten up. Allie, take a couple deep breaths. We are almost to the fountain."

The Spywells' car finally turned onto a wide avenue, leaving the red Cadillac's side as it sped off along the waterway. Before them a huge white marble fountain stood in the middle of the road.

The road circled around the fountain. Mr. Spywell pulled the car up alongside the curb and parked. Allie quickly threw open the car door and let the cool breeze from the straits fill her lungs. Breathe deep, breathe deep, she repeated over and over to herself. When she felt like she could stand, she carefully crawled out of the car onto the sidewalk. Slowly she straightened up and stretched. She began to feel better.

"I just needed to get out of that car and stop going in circles. That red car was making me sick, too, bouncing along beside us like that," she explained.

Shoo pushed Allie aside as he crawled out her side of the car. He stood and stretched like a cat in the afternoon sun. "I just needed to get away from you," he teased his sister.

Mrs. Spywell took their camera from its case and handed it to her husband as he opened a fresh roll of film. "This is great," she said. "I want to get pictures of Allie and Shoo sitting at the edge of the fountain by old **Neptune**. I have pictures my mother and dad took of me sitting in the same spot over thirty years ago. I think it would be neat to compare them."

Allie and Shoo waited while their father loaded the camera. They knew their mom and dad took gazillions of pictures every place in the world they traveled. They had albums and albums of pictures that were fun to look at on cold winter nights. Allie stood silently, breathing deep to allow her stomach to settle, when all of a sudden Shoo whacked her on the back and ran down the sidewalk towards the fountain. "Come on, let's go, sickie!" he yelled. "You're all right."

Shoo ran as fast as he could, pausing at the marble steps leading to the fountain. He looked back and waved his hand to Allie to hurry up. Turning, he caught his toe on the worn marble steps and tripped over his feet.

Allie watched and laughed at her clumsy

brother. What a clown, she thought.

Shoo picked himself up and looked back to see if his parents had noticed. He saw they were still busy loading the camera, so he was safe.

Allie walked quickly and caught up with her brother. Her stomach was better now. At the top of the steps, the bright blue sky outlined a beautiful white, three-tiered, marble fountain. It was huge and was filled with large lions and small turtles all spouting water. Dolphin statues sprang from a pool that encircled the fountain.

This is cool! thought Allie.

There beside the fountain was a life-size bronze statue of a seated man looking downriver towards the tall buildings of Detroit.

"That's Jim Scott," said their mother as she joined them. "He's the man that gave his estate in 1910 to have this fountain built. He really liked Belle Isle, but the people of Detroit didn't like him very much."

"Why not?" questioned Shoo.

"Well, the story goes that Mr. Scott inherited his money from his wealthy father and he never worked a day in his entire life. He liked to have fun, play cards, gamble, and play tricks on people. When he died, he wanted to give his estate to build this fountain so the city would remember him. The people of the city weren't sure they wanted to remember him."

"Well, I'm glad they decided to take his money. This fountain is really cool," commented Shoo.

"Yeah," added Allie, "and people will always have to remember Jim Scott as long as he is sitting there staring at Detroit. I wonder what he is thinking about?"

Just then a spray of cool water from a

spouting turtle caught in the breeze and blew against Allie and Shoo. The little spatters were cold and made them both jump and shiver. "Maybe he is trying to tell you something," laughed their mother.

"Hey, you two. . ." said Mr. Spywell as he joined his family in front of the fountain toting the camera. "Your mother wants a picture of you both sitting in front of old Neptune over there." Their father motioned as he waved them around to the other side of the fountain. Allie and Shoo followed and soon stood at the rim of a huge basin of water. "Okay, smile," instructed their father as he held up the camera and focused the lens. "Say 'history!'" SNAP! "Okay, now let's get another one with your mom in it, too." All three gathered together and squinted a "history" smile towards the camera as Mr. Spywell took another picture.

"There we have it. Another memory

caught in time and another story to tell," he said. Mrs. Spywell grinned at her husband because she knew how much he loved to tell stories, just as she did.

"You know I remember this place when I was young and growing up," reminisced Mrs. Spywell. "My parents used to bring a picnic lunch over here and we would always visit this fountain. I would sit in that very same spot and try to splash old Neptune."

"Has this place always been a park?" questioned Allie.

"As long as I can remember," said her mother.

"When the Indians were here a long time ago, they used to call this place White Swan Island," said their father.

"Oh boy, here we go again," complained Shoo as he rolled his eyes. "More history stuff."

"It was also called Hog Island," added

their mother. "There are lots of stories about Belle Isle and Detroit, many of them mysterious ones—actually weird, as Shoo likes to say. No wonder I always wanted to be a writer when I was a kid. I grew up hearing these great stories," she said.

CHAPTER

Weird Stories

"I know a good snake story about this place," interrupted Mr. Spywell.

"I'll let your father tell the story. You know how he loves to tell stories, and I am sure he will include history."

Shoo moaned as if in pain and Allie rolled her eyes. Here we go again, she thought.

Mr. Spywell smiled, the camera hanging loosely on the strap around his neck. "Well, **archaeologists** and **geologists** know that a long time ago, this river used to be very deep. Of course, the river changed after the glaciers had done their work and melted, some 10,000 years ago. It became similar to what we see today. The **Algonquian-**

speaking Indians used the narrows to get to their hunting and trapping grounds. Then the Iroquois used it as a warpath."

"Dad?" said Shoo.

"In the 1600s the Iroquois were friends with the Dutch who founded New Amsterdam, which is now New York," continued Mr. Spywell. "The Dutch were involved with the fur trade, and the Iroquois supplied them with tons of furs to ship back to Europe to make hats, **cloaks**, and ornaments."

"Dad?" said Shoo again.

"When the beaver of New York were depleted, the Iroquois pushed up into the Great Lakes, trying to destroy tribes like the **Neutrals**, the **Huron**, and Algonquin tribes like the **Odawa** and **Ojibwa**, and planning to steal their fur.

"The English took over from the Dutch, made friends with the Iroquois, and gave them guns and supplies to push even further into the Great Lakes. They used this strait as their roadway for destruction. Isn't that interesting?" asked their father.

Both the children laughed and shook their heads "NO" at the same time.

"What about the snakes? That's just history! I want to hear about snakes," said Shoo.

Mr. Spywell frowned at Shoo and continued. "About 1670 a French priest named **Father Dollier** landed along the Detroit River, somewhere between the mouth of the **Rouge River** and old **Fort Wayne**. He made a huge wooden cross that had the French **coat of arms** on it. But he planted the cross on the very site of an ancient Indian **shrine**, destroying a stone figure that had been worshipped by the Indians for generations."

"Well, that wasn't very nice," commented Allie.

"What about the snakes? I want snakes," insisted Shoo.

"In 1679 **La Salle** also came through these straits in the *Griffin,* the first sailing ship ever to be seen on the Great Lakes."

Allie looked at her brother, her eyes opened wide. "You mean La Salle's ghost ship, the *Griffin*?"

"That's the one!" agreed their father.

"What about the snakes? Snakes! Snakes!" demanded Shoo.

"It was La Salle that named **Lake St. Clair**, because he crossed it on the feast day of St. Claire. And Shoo, don't ask me again about snakes. I am getting there."

"Oh, Lake St. Clair is a beautiful lake," added Mrs. Spywell. "I used to go sailing there with my father when I was young."

Shoo, bored by his father's history lesson and his mother's memories, shook his head and crossed his arms over his chest. I knew this was going to happen, he thought.

"Did you ever see the snake creatures that were supposed to live in the waters there?" asked Mr. Spywell with a grin to his wife.

Shoo looked at Allie and smiled. It might take a while, he thought, but his father always did get to the good stuff.

"Yeah, snakes!" added Shoo, rubbing his hands together. "It's about time!"

Mrs. Spywell snickered and shook her head. "No, I don't think so." She looked at Shoo and Allie. "I think your father is exaggerating now."

"No, really. Around the 1890s people kept spotting these weird, snake-like creatures in the lake and in the straits. They were very long with snake-like bodies, heads like bulls, but with only one eye."

"Sounds like Shoo," said Allie.

"Be quiet," snapped Shoo as he nudged

his sister. "This is finally getting interesting."

"A group of people from around Lake St. Clair," continued Mr. Spywell, "even named the thing—or things."

"Really?" wondered Mrs. Spywell. "And what name might that be?"

"They called the creature Clair-A-Belle."

"Oh, brother," said Allie, "Clair-A-Belle." She and her mother started to laugh.

"Leave Dad alone. This is a cool story," protested Shoo. "This is what a cryptozoologist does, studies weird creatures."

"Maybe you better look in the mirror," said Allie with a giggle.

"You know," continued their father and ignoring Allie's remark, "they even said that one of those creatures made it up to Belle Isle where it was caught by a ship's captain. He said it had a mouth as big as a shovel and was hissing and sputtering through the water at a great rate of speed. It was even reported in the Detroit *News-Tribune*, an old newspaper of that time."

"Well, if that were really true," interrupted Mrs. Spywell, "where did the creatures go? I was raised in Detroit, and I've never seen one. No one I ever knew talked about seeing them either."

Mr. Spywell looked at his wife in surprise. "You don't believe me, do you? It was written up in the newspaper in 1897. I thought you loved a mystery—and this is a real mystery. According to the story, the people along the straits chased the creatures south until they were forced to flee into Lake Erie."

"Oh, let me get this right. So the creatures live in Lake Erie now?" asked Mrs. Spywell as she lifted her eyebrows and smiled sweetly at her husband.

"I guess," said Mr. Spywell who quickly looked down at his shoes. "There are just a lot of strange stories about Detroit and these waterways."

"Well, what about the factual stories? I am sure we would all enjoy hearing more about history," commented Mrs. Spywell.

"Mom!" moaned Shoo. "I thought you were on our side. You are supposed to like weird stories like that."

"Mom's right," agreed Allie, just to bug her brother. "History and facts teach you something. But you wouldn't know about that, would you?"

Shoo scrunched up his face at his sister. "You think you are so smart, Allie," he muttered under his breath.

"Well," continued their father, "since you want to hear more about history, you need to know that on July 19th, 1701, the Iroquois gave a huge amount of land all around what is now the city of Detroit to the English, even though it wasn't theirs to give. And five days later, on July 24, **Sieur Antoine de la Mothe Cadillac** arrived here with about twenty-five canoes and a hundred men, including soldiers, workmen, and **voyageurs**. They claimed the land all over again, this time for France. After that, they cleared an acre of land and built Fort Pontchartrain down by the river. They called it *Ville d'Etroit*, or the Village of the Straits. They selected the location because it had at that time a high bank where they could see down on any enemy ship that might be trying to pass through the narrows. Then they could fire their cannons at it from the fort."

"Cool," said Shoo. "You said, Punch-a-train? How do you Punch-a-train?" Wouldn't you get run over?"

"Count Pontchartrain," corrected his

mother, "was the name of the French Governor that backed Cadillac. Today a huge hotel stands on the very spot where the fort was built. And do you know what else is weird? Because there are so many strange stories about old Detroit, Hotel Pontchartrain doesn't even have a thirteenth floor listed on their elevator. I know, because I've been there."

"What?" questioned Shoo. "Let me get this straight. Do they have thirteen floors in that hotel?"

"There are many more floors than thirteen, Shoo. It's a big hotel," explained his father.

"Okay, more than thirteen floors, but no thirteenth floor? What holds the fourteenth floor up?" he asked.

"Shoo, don't be silly. Floor number fourteen," explained his mother, "is really the thirteenth floor."

"What? That doesn't make sense," said Shoo.

"It doesn't take much for you, does it Shoo?" laughed Allie as she shook her head. "It's **superstition**, you know, the number thirteen is supposed to be bad luck. So they don't use the number thirteen for a floor in their hotel because it is bad luck. Duh."

"Wow, that's weird," he said as he thought about a big hotel being afraid to have a thirteenth floor.

"Anyway," continued their father, "Cadillac convinced the king of France, **Louis XIV,** that the straits was the key to the upper Great Lakes. It gave New France the best access to the **Mississippi Valley**, which La Salle and **Marquette** had opened. Cadillac knew if the English seized the straits, the French fur trade would be ruined."

"How could the Iroquois give land to the

English that wasn't theirs?" asked Allie.

"Allie! Dad! No more history! More weird stories," complained Shoo. "I want to hear more about snakes and creatures. You said there were lots of weird stories and that's what I want to hear about."

"Shoo," said his father. "Have you ever really looked at the spelling of the word history? Do you know the biggest part of that word is the word 'story'? So all these stories come together making Detroit's past really come alive."

"Yeah, but I like weird stuff."

"All you have to do is look in a mirror to see weird," said Allie.

Shoo pushed hard against his sister's arm. "You're not very nice, you know that?"

Allie shook her head and walked away. Mrs. Spywell, standing on the steps of the fountain, looked down at her watch. "Hey, if we are going to get to the Detroit His-

30

torical Museum before it closes, we'd better get a move on. We can finish the stories in the car."

3

CHAPTER

Detroit Historical Museum

Shoo raced down the marble steps and over the sidewalk heading towards the car. Allie watched and wondered if he would fall again.

At the car, Allie smiled as he tried, unsuccessfully, to open the doors. The car was locked. He just wanted to pick the best seat for himself, she thought. He always did.

"Allie, would you like to sit up front with your father?" asked her mother as they approached the car. " I'll sit in the back with Shoo."

Overhearing, Shoo blurted out, "Hey, no fair! I was here first!"

Allie smiled, "Would it be all right, Mom?" She grinned sweetly at her brother.

"Sure. You didn't feel very well riding in the back of this little car, and I don't want you to get carsick again. I want you to enjoy the museum."

"No fair," whispered Shoo.

Allie hopped into the front seat beside her father and fastened her seat belt. She pulled down the sun-visor and glanced in the mirror at her brother, who sat staring out the car window with a frown on his face.

"Now Shoo, you still want to hear more stories?" asked their father as he snapped on his seat belt and started up the car.

"I do if they're weird."

"They're weird, all right," said Mr. Spywell as he drove the car slowly around the island. They passed the **botanic gardens** and soccer fields, then cut across to the road leading over the bridge and turned left onto Jefferson Avenue.

"A long time ago before the French arrived, Belle Isle was covered with snakes."

"Yuck. Snakes, again?" said Allie.

"Hey," interrupted Shoo. "You think that creature, that Clair-A-Belle, was just a big snake originally from Belle Isle?"

"Could be. Well, anyway, there was also a small tribe of Odawa Indians who lived there. Their chief was named Sleeping Bear, and he had a daughter that was said to be so beautiful that she had a strange magical power over everyone that looked at her. The chief was afraid of his daughter's beauty, so he put her in a **birch bark canoe** and **moored** it out on the Detroit River. He covered it with woven mats to protect her from the weather and to keep anyone passing by from seeing her beauty."

"That's not fair," said Allie. "Just because she was beautiful? There is nothing wrong with that." Allie ran her fingers through her hair and stuck her nose up into the air.

"It's just a story, Allie. Listen," added her mother.

"Yeah, listen and don't interrupt. What would you know about beauty anyway?" teased Shoo.

"Well," continued their father, "one day the warm summer Wind was blowing from the south. He just happened to blow so hard that he blew the mats off from the top of the birch bark canoe that the girl was living in.

"The Wind was so taken by the girl's beauty that he blew even stronger to impress her. He blew so hard that he snapped the mooring ropes that held the canoe secure.

"The Keeper of the Water-Gates, a red **gnome**-like creature with horns and a long tail, heard the cries of the girl and rescued her from the canoe and the Wind.

"He too was impressed by her beauty and

took the girl to his wigwam. The Wind, jealous of what the Keeper had done, blew hard against the wigwam until he blew it over and the Keeper escaped. The Wind returned the girl to her father and instructed him never to hide her beauty again, but to let her live on the island in freedom."

"Belle Isle?" asked Allie.

"Yes, Belle Isle, but it was called White Swan Island then. To protect the girl from any evil, her father prayed to the **Great Manitou** to send her protection. The Manitou sent snakes to surround the girl and keep her safe."

"Cool, more snakes," smiled Shoo.

"When Cadillac came to Detroit in 1701, it was said there were so many snakes on the island that only hogs could live there, since hogs will kill and eat snakes. Also, putting the hogs on the island kept them safe from the wolves that inhabited the mainland."

"So the French put their hogs there to eat the snakes?" questioned Shoo.

"And to keep the hogs safe from the wolves. The island went from being called White Swan Island to Hog Island and finally to Belle Isle."

"I didn't see any bells on the island," commented Shoo. "Why do they call it Bell Isle?"

"No, not that kind of bell. The word B-E-L-L-E is French for beautiful," explained their mother.

"Like the beautiful Indian girl who once lived there," added Allie. "Whatever happened to her?"

"As the story goes," continued their father, "her spirit still lives on the island and that is why it has remained beautiful for so long."

"What happened to the red gnome that

disappeared?" asked Shoo.

"Some say when his lodge was blown down he escaped and moved to *Peche* (Peach) Island, an island upriver."

"There's a story about the great Odawa chief Pontiac and this creature," added Mrs. Spywell. "The story goes that before Chief Pontiac started his rebellion against the British in the 1760s, he went to visit Peche Island, seeking the advice of the red gnome who became known as the **oracle**. The gnome advised Chief Pontiac to drive everyone, except Native Americans, from these lands. And with that advice, **Pontiac's Rebellion** began."

"I didn't know that story," commented their father. "I do know that Cadillac was supposed to be haunted by the red gnome. He believed that the red gnome stole Detroit from him."

"I know that story, too," agreed their

mother. "I was doing online research and ran across an old newspaper article with that story in it. Cadillac called it the *Nain Rouge*, French for Red Gnome."

"That sounds cool," remarked Shoo. "Tell the story."

"Before I tell the story, I want you to look at this big building coming up. It's Hotel Pontchartrain."

Allie and Shoo looked up at the tall skyscraper and its huge glass windows as their father drove around the corner. It's really big," commented Shoo. "I don't see an empty space for the thirteenth floor."

"Here, on this very spot, is where Cadillac built his fort, the first French settlement of the straits, *Ville d'Etroit*."

"So what happened to the fort?" asked Shoo as they drove past the building. "Is it inside the hotel?"

"No," said Mrs. Spywell as she looked

out the window at the skyscraper. "Some storytellers say that the fort and almost all of Detroit was destroyed by the Nain Rouge. They believed that the Red Gnome tried to chase the French off the ancient lands of the Indians."

"Are you saying some weird creature was really part of Detroit's history?" Allie scrunched her face in disbelief.

"No, Allie." Her father shook his head. "Those are just stories, legends to explain what happened and why. In truth, there were many problems in starting the new settlement, and Cadillac made a number of enemies in his dealings. In 1710 he was removed from command and sent on to Louisiana."

"When people don't have information or knowledge, they tend to be superstitious," her mother added. "Then these superstitions are woven into some pretty strange stories."

"Sooo," Allie continued, "how am I supposed to know which stories in history are true and which are not?"

"Just ask your father," Mr. Spywell grinned.

Allie sighed and turned her attention to the city they were slowly moving through.

"This sure is a big city," said Shoo as they passed tall buildings, construction cranes, and hundreds of people walking along the streets.

"People from almost every country in the world live here and in the surrounding area," said Mr. Spywell.

"Was it big 300 years ago?" asked Shoo.

"No, it takes time for a city to grow to be this big and for buildings to be built," answered their father.

Allie and Shoo watched out the car windows thinking about what this place might have looked like 300 years ago.

Allie imagined a deep, dark forest covered with trees and surrounded by miles of wilderness. Shoo thought about the Indians that lived here and the wild howling wolves that roamed the woods.

"Hey, here we are," said their father as he turned down a short street. "Detroit Historical Museum. Kids, look over there," he pointed to a building across the street. "That building is the **Detroit Public Library**. I've done lots of research there."

"The Burton Historical Collection is housed there, too," commented their mother. "It's a great place to do research."

"All libraries are great," added their father.

Allie smiled. She knew how much her parents loved books and history. Although she complained about their endless history lessons, she loved that they were both so smart.

Their father quickly parked their car and they all hurried to the museum. Shoo and Allie walked ahead to the entrance as a large group of school children with several adults exited. Inside the door, the security man behind the desk in the lobby called to them.

"The museum will be closing in about an hour, folks. You will need to hurry if you want to see the exhibits."

"We will, thank you," said Mrs. Spywell smiling at the security guard.

"I want to go see the Motor City exhibit," said their father. "Maybe they have an old Cadillac or some pictures on display. Shoo? Allie? You want to come with me?" he asked as they all started up the stairs.

"I really think Shoo and Allie should go downstairs and see the Streets of Old Detroit exhibit. It's really fascinating, with brick streets and old store fronts. Next time we come, you can take them to check out the car exhibit."

"Mom," moaned Shoo.

"You will like the Old Detroit exhibit and we haven't got time to argue. Let's go," she insisted.

As they reached the top of the stairs a great old clock standing in the corner started to chime off the hours. More than fifteen feet tall, the clock was the biggest Allie and Shoo had ever seen. A sign beside it read, Louis Meier Clock. It was over fifteen feet tall.

"Wow, that sure would make a great alarm clock," joked Shoo as he turned to his mother. "Oh no, I knew it. Look, Allie, Mom is in the gift shop looking at books."

Shoo and Allie entered the gift shop and watched their mother take one book down from the shelf and then another.

"Mom." Allie and Shoo stood patiently

until their mother noticed them.

"Why don't you two go ahead and go downstairs and see the exhibit. I will be right down. Just follow the steps. Did you see where your father went towards the car exhibit?" Allie and Shoo caught sight of their father as he disappeared through an entryway.

"The steps are right there. I'll be down in just a few minutes, as soon as I am done looking."

Shoo darted out of the gift shop, past a woman working behind a counter, to the area where his father had disappeared. There he found a dimly lit stairway leading down. Allie watched Shoo and followed. Shoo better go downstairs and not into the car exhibit, she thought to herself.

By the time Allie found the stairwell, she could hear Shoo's feet racing down the marble steps ahead of her. She listened for

him to fall. Show-off, she thought. He just wants to be the first one to the exhibit.

The stairway was kind of spooky and dim, and the museum was really quiet. No one was around except for the security guard and the worker in the gift shop.

Allie stood at the top of the marble stairs looking down towards a landing and a dark doorway. There on the landing sat a very large old trunk and a **mannequin** dressed in a fancy French gown. In the doorway to the exhibit, Allie could see a dim red light glowing. Strange, she thought.

Just then, from the deep mouth of the doorway, she heard a low, growly voice, "Allie. . . Allie. . . come into the streets of old Detroit. I am waiting for you. Ha, ha, ha, haaaaa."

"Shoo, you're such a jerk," she called down the stairs to him. "Stop goofing around. You're in a museum."

Shoo popped his head around the dark doorway and started to laugh. "Come on down. It's really neat, like an old city with a hotel front, a bike shop, street lights and everything. Hurry up."

"Just go on and leave me alone," she snapped as Shoo disappeared through the door.

4

The Ghost

Carefully, one step at a time, Allie made her way down the marble steps towards the landing, holding tightly onto the handrail. As she took her last step, the silent mannequin sitting on the old trunk moved ever so slightly. Allie jumped. What she thought was not living, now seemed alive. She watched wide-eyed and silent as the seated form breathed deeply and sighed.

Allie laughed at herself. This wasn't a mannequin at all! How could she have made that mistake?

Just then the woman in the fancy gown reached out a graceful hand and straightened the folds of her long full skirt and again sighed deeply. Allie tried hard not to stare or be rude. Either the woman was very sad, or bored with her job, Allie decided.

As she passed by the woman, Allie could not help but take another glance. The woman's eyes were bright blue, and they seemed to be glowing like Christmas tree bulbs. She had tears running down her cheeks.

Suddenly the woman looked up and stared right into Allie's eyes. Startled and unsure about what to do, Allie smiled. The woman seemed to look right through Allie, searching the stairwell as if looking for something or someone.

"*Qui est là*? (Who's there?) Is there someone there?" whispered the woman in a deep rich accent.

Perhaps she's blind, thought Allie as she cleared her throat to respond.

"*C'est qui*? (Who is it?) Is it you, you nasty one? Is it you?" she said in a loud, demanding voice.

Allie thought for a minute. She had never been called nasty before, and she wondered if she should feel insulted. She must think I am someone else, decided Allie.

Allie gathered her courage and cleared her throat again. "Hi," she said. "Are you all right? Do you need some help?" Allie asked politely.

"Who is there? I hear you, but I do not see your face, you evil one! Go from me and leave me in peace," said the woman. This time she reached out as if searching for someone in the dark.

The woman continued. "Is that you? You are so cruel. Will you never leave me and my family alone?"

Allie looked up the stairway, now sure that the woman must be speaking to someone else. But there was no one else there!

Uncertain about what to say, Allie again

tried to offer help. "Hi. My name's Allie. Do you need help?" she asked politely.

The woman burst into tears. "It is you! You are an evil one. Is it not enough you have robbed my husband of the glory that was his? Must you haunt me forever?" she cried. "*Pourquoi*? (Why?) Why don't you just leave me alone? It has been so long. Why don't you just go away, you evil one, so I may join my loved ones?"

Allie leaned back against the handrail as the woman stood. "I cannot see you, but I am not afraid. Do you hear me? Not afraid! I will keep the name and memory of my husband alive until you leave or are destroyed."

Haunt? Destroyed? Oh no. Not again, thought Allie, as the woman reached out with her hands and grabbed at the air around her. Allie tried to duck away, but the woman caught her arm.

The instant the woman touched Allie, icy goosebumps, like needles, ran up and down Allie's arm, and the hair on the back of her neck stood stiff. Allie could even feel goosebumps on the top of her head. Suddenly, she noticed her arm beginning to glow where the woman had grabbed her. It turned a soft, fuzzy bluish-white color while the woman's hand that held her pulsated in an iridescent blue.

OH NO! thought Allie. What's happening?

Just then a cool wind swirled around the two and a bluish-white light encircled them as they stood on the landing. Allie could feel sparks of **magnetic charges** all around her, like tiny rubber bands snapping her skin. At the same time she felt herself pulled closer to the woman, like a magnet toward metal.

Struggling, Allie tried to pull away, but

it was no use. She and the woman were locked together in a strange glowing space. Shocks of static electricity snapped Allie's arms and face and the wind blew even harder around the two. Allie's hair stood on end with the wind and static electricity. The woman tried to look at Allie while shielding her face from the wind.

"Who are you? Where did you come from?" The woman shrieked in terror and tried to pull away, as if Allie was the one holding her.

"Who am I? Who are *you*?" shouted Allie in the roar of the wind. "Let go of me!" she cried as she tried to pull and squirm away from the woman's electric touch.

"Shoo! Shoo, help me!" Allie hollered frantically for her brother.

Instantly the wind stopped whirling and Allie's hair fell back into place. The woman was now able let go and fell backward to her seat on the trunk. But a bluish-white glowing bubble now held them captive—together.

"How cruel! How cruel you are, appearing before me as a child to remind me of my family. What do you want with me? Tell me. I demand it!" yelled the woman at Allie.

"What are you talking about?" yelled Allie back. "I'm not cruel. I'm just Allie." Allie tried to move as far away from the woman as she could, but the hazy, light seemed to seal them in like an invisible wall. "Shoo!" she cried again for her brother.

The woman on the trunk stared intently at Allie for a moment. Her glowing blue eyes softened and glistened with tears. "Why do you haunt me so?"

"What are you talking about?" shouted Allie. "Why can't I move? Let me go!" demanded Allie as she tried and tried to pull away from the power of the light that held them together. "Do you hear me? Let me go!"

The woman on the trunk fearfully reached her hand out again towards Allie. Allie tried to move away.

"*S'il vous plait* (Please)," said the woman in a soft voice. The delicate lace of her sleeve fell forward over her ghostly hand, and pale, icy-blue fingers touched Allie's warm skin. Again, goosebumps ran up and down Allie's arms as the ghostly figure pulled back her frozen hand and began to wail. Her sorrowful cries echoed up the stairway.

Where's Shoo? Why can't he hear what's going on? wondered Allie.

"*Non! Non!* (No! No!) How can this be? A human child brought to me now? What have I done? I am so sorry, my child. What have I done?

"I have given up the company of all to

be certain the spirit of my husband, Sieur Antoine de la Mothe Cadillac, is not forgotten in le Détroit, the place where his glorious dreams were being built and then were stolen by the evil one. It is the place where Nain Rouge has done his best to destroy the memory of my great, dear husband."

Allie was shocked by the words of this haunted woman. Nain Rouge? Why did that sound familiar? Wasn't Nain Rouge the name her mother called that red gnome thing? thought Allie. Allie watched great pale tears roll down the French woman's ghostly white cheeks.

"Don't cry. Everything will be all right." Allie was surprised to find herself trying to comfort the woman.

The woman shook her head. Carefully she lifted the lace of her sleeve, reached into the deep blue fabric, and pulled out an embroidered hanky. As she waved the hanky in the air to straighten it, Allie could smell a sweet lilac scent fill the landing. The woman dabbed her cheeks softly and lightly wiped her nose.

How elegant, thought Allie. Who is this woman?

Just then, Shoo popped his head around the doorway and looked up the staircase. It looked as if his face was peering right into the bluish-white bubble, but he didn't even seem to notice.

"Shoo!" yelled Allie. "Where have you been? Check this out! This lady, she. . . ."

Shoo walked up beside the trunk. "Geeze, what's that weird smell?" he said. "It smells like flowers or something." He sniffed the air and then called up the stairs. "Allie? Allie? Where are you?"

"What are you talking about?" snapped Allie. "I'm standing right beside you, you dufus!" Allie stretched out her hand to touch her brother's face. But her hand disappeared right into him.

Shoo stood frozen to the spot for a moment and looked around the landing. He reached out towards the trunk and his hand passed right through the fabric of the woman's skirt.

Shoo shivered. "That's weird. It's cold right here," he said quietly to himself. "And what's that smell? Where's Allie?"

"Shoo!" Allie called her brother's name as loudly as she could right into his ear. "What's the matter with you? Why can't you see me?" she cried.

Shoo paused as if listening to something far away in the distance.

"Allie?" he called up the stairs again. "Stop fooling around! This is really neat down here. There's this kid here, too. He's really cool." A short boy with a red cap

pulled down low over his forehead suddenly appeared out of the darkened exhibit room behind Shoo.

The woman on the trunk pulled back in fear, holding her hanky over her mouth. "*Non!*" she cried.

As the boy came closer, Allie could see he was wearing a jean jacket and pants and red tennis shoes. He looked directly at the woman and smiled. He almost acts like he can see her, thought Allie. The woman covered her eyes with her pale hands and hanky.

"That's weird," said Shoo to the boy. "Allie was here just a minute ago. She must have gone back upstairs to the bookstore. Come on, let's go get her. She can't miss this. The Streets of Old Detroit is really neat."

Allie tried grabbing Shoo's arm, but her hand again disappeared into his flesh. Shoo stopped and shivered. "It's really cold right here," he commented as he went up the marble stairs with his new friend right behind him. As the boy passed Allie, he gave her a sly smile.

Allie was startled. He sees us, she thought, but why can't Shoo?

The boy then turned back to the woman. His smile turned into a snarl, and his teeth suddenly looked pointed. He made a sound that seemed to Allie to be a hiss. "What kind of weirdo are you?" blurted Allie as she watched the boy's **transformation**.

The woman began to weep loudly, and Allie found herself beginning to panic. "Shoo!" she called as she watched her brother climb the stairs with the creature-boy close behind.

The Promise

"Shoo! Shoo!" cried Allie. "Why can't he hear me? Why can't he see me!" Allie begged the woman to answer.

Peeking through the spaces between her fingers, the woman watched as Shoo and the creature disappeared up the stairs and through the doorway.

Gathering her courage the woman said slowly, "It is the evil Nain Rouge."

Allie had calmed herself and shook her head. "That's just my brother, Shoo, and some weird kid in red tennis shoes."

"*Non!* It is the spirit of Nain Rouge, and your brother—he is in grave danger."

"I'm not afraid!" snapped Allie. "Shoo and I have had plenty of strange things happen to us. Everything is going to be okay. Who are you anyway?" she demanded.

The woman stood and straightened the folds of her long, fancy dress. She carefully folded her hanky and slid it up underneath the lace on her sleeve. "*Je m' appelle* (my name is) Marie-Thérèse Guyon (Gee-on) Cadillac. Madame Cadillac. The wife of the most honorable Antoine de la Mothe Cadillac, founder of *le Détroit*."

With this introduction, the woman daintily lifted the sides of her long skirt and curtsied like Allie had seen in the movies.

"What? How can you be Madame Cadillac? Madame Cadillac died long ago."

The woman cast her eyes sideways toward Allie. "You are very rude for one so young. You ask questions of me, and I do not even know your name. You may address me as Madame or Madame Cadillac, whichever suits you. *Et vous?* (And you?)"

"Me? I'm Allie, Allie Spywell, and that first boy going up the stairs, the one without the weird pointed teeth, that's my brother Shoo. What are you doing here? And why doesn't that boy-creature like you?"

"That is the wicked Nain Rouge, as my husband called him, the red gnome. It followed him from the moment he first arrived here on July 24, in the year of our Lord 1701."

Madame Cadillac began to relive her memories with Allie. "Ah, my husband had such hopes for this place. He wrote letters back to me telling of this land and of its great beauty.

"He chose this site himself, as the climate at the straits of Mackinac was too severe for his liking. But here, south of the pearl-like lake, Lake St. Clair, at a place the Odawas called Crooked Bend, he would build a great city. These were his very words.

"'On both banks,' he wrote, 'stretched fine open plains where roamed herds of graceful deer, bear, and wild duck, and fifteen **leagues** (forty-five miles) from here, buffalo roamed in great abundance, and every variety of game was to be found.'

"He also wrote that the grass was so high a man could barely be seen walking in it."

"Wow, that's long grass," said Allie.

"*Oui*. And in the river, he wrote, were 'islands covered with fruit trees, and in the fall the wild grape vines could scarcely hold up their sweet burden.' This fair locality, this paradise, he named *le Détroit*.

"It was the gateway of *les Grands Lacs* (Great Lakes), the one spot best suited to hold *l'Anglais* (the English) back.

"My husband was so brave, he told everyone his new settlement would grow to rival **Montreal**. He said it would be a miracle on the **frontier**."

"Didn't you come here with your husband? " asked Allie.

"*Non*, he came ahead to make a home
for me and the children. I missed him very
much when we were apart. . .just as I miss
him now.

"My husband needed me at his side, but
it was important to him that we first have a
safe home for the children.

"He once wrote that there were only a
few things a person had to fear here; they
were the long hard winters filled with cold,
wind, and snow. But I was raised in **Quebec**, *une femme Nouveau Monde* (a woman
of the New World). I was accustomed to
the harsh life and nothing could be as long
and cold as the winters in Quebec.

"Another fear was the fierce Iroquois that
were friends with *l'Anglais*. But my husband
was so charming, he was making peace with

these people. And with his many skills it would not take him long to negotiate and smoke the pipe of peace with them. A peace that would bring my husband, Antoine, much honor and **acclaim** from good King Louis.

"The last enemy was loneliness. The men did not have their wives beside them. This enemy of loneliness is something very powerful. I know it well.

"My husband was always practical. It was important to him that I joined him only when it was safe, and I was able. And that other wives and families should follow as soon as it was possible. He knew a new settlement must have familes, not just rough fur traders.

"I would join Antoine in the wilderness and stand at his side and live in our new home to serve as an example to other women of New France, proving that *le*

Détroit was safe for them and their babies.

"When he first arrived, my husband brought our nine-year-old son Antoine to teach him the ways of the great explorers, the fur traders, and the voyageurs. My husband with his soldiers and the workmen built a great fort not far from here."

"Fort Pontchartrain," interrupted Allie.

"*Oui*. Of course, you have been to the fort?" questioned Madame Cadillac with pleasure.

"Well, no. It's not there any more. It's a hotel now."

"Oh, another thing built by my husband's hands that has been lost and forgotten!" Madame cried as she slowly pulled her hanky from beneath her lacy sleeve and blew her nose.

"The fort was built to keep the glory of France alive in this region and to stop the invasion of the devious *l'Anglais* who wanted to take *le commerce des fourrures* (the fur trade). Ah! Nain Rouge at his cruel work!"

"But didn't Nain Rouge live on Peche Island?" asked Allie.

"He is very ancient. He first lived here before there was anyone, even before the Indians. He guarded the straits and protected the land."

"The Keeper of the Water-Gates," said Allie. "My dad told us that story. He tried to steal the beautiful daughter of Chief Sleeping Bear and was almost destroyed by the Wind, but he escaped to Peche Island where he was an oracle to the Native Americans. He wanted them to drive out all the foreigners from the land." Allie thought how pleased her father would be to hear her repeat the story.

"*Oui*, he is the one. But he wanted more than to drive them away. He also wanted to destroy the memory of the man, my husband, who built this great settlement.

"He did everything he could to destroy my husband and his memory. That is why I have pledged to stay here for an eternity if I must, to keep alive the memory of my husband in this place of his stolen dreams. *Vive le Seigneur Cadillac du Détroit!* (Long live Sir Cadillac of Detroit!)" Madame called loudly and waved her lilac scented hanky in the air.

"It was Nain Rouge that caused my husband to lose his position and his lands. It was his doing that we were forced to go to France to live and die, away from the place we loved.

"When I was very old I vowed to return to this place in spirit to keep alive the memory of Antoine de la Mothe Cadillac and protect this city of his dreams as best I could from the power of Nain Rouge—at least until Nain Rouge was driven away or destroyed."

"How long have you been here?" asked Allie.

"As long as memories are old," replied Madame Cadillac with a sad look. "I have been here and alone, it seems, forever."

Allie felt the loneliness of the woman as she dropped her head and tears, again, ran down her pale cheeks. Allie couldn't imagine living in a stairway landing—even as a ghost—so people would not forget her husband. She must have really loved him, Allie decided.

6

The Arrival

Allie touched the woman's cold hand, trying to comfort her. Again goosebumps shot up Allie's arms. Madame Cadillac looked at Allie and smiled at her warm touch.

"I am so sorry that I brought you here. I do not know how it happened. It must be Nain Rouge again, trying to play tricks on me. He does that just to show me how forgotten my life is, and that of my husband and family."

"But you really aren't forgotten," said Allie hoping to cheer her up.

Madame Cadillac shook her head and looked down.

Trying to change the subject, Allie asked,

"If you didn't come with your husband to Detroit, when did you arrive?"

Madame looked up, her blue eyes sparkled with a sudden flash of memory from long ago.

"I arrived here from Quebec in early spring in the year of our Lord 1702. I traveled with my husband's voyageurs and *mon ami* (my friend) Marie-Anne, the wife of Alphonse de Tonty, my husband's second in command at *le Détroit*. She was my only woman friend in the wilderness.

"We left Quebec in birch bark canoes. Our six-year-old son Jacques was with me. He was *un gentil garcon* (a good boy) on the trip. We traveled along *la Riviere Laurent* (the St. Lawrence River) to *Lac Frontenac* (Lake Ontario), and *Lac Erié*. We traveled 250 leagues (750 miles) in six weeks. I left behind our eldest son, Joseph, and two daughters, Madeleine and Judith. It was best for the girls to live in a convent and be educated to become proper ladies.

"My guilt haunts me today when I think back how very much afraid I was. I knew my place was with the company of my husband, but it was so far away from civilization! How could I bear it? So far from the pretty streets of Quebec. So far from my mama and papa. So far away from all I knew. But I was needed to set the example for other women to follow in my footsteps and settle here at this place—the place that was to rival Montreal!

"Women are the ones that remind men of who they are. They remind them to keep of good cheer, to attend church, and to take care of their family. Wives keep their men honest. Wives plant roots to raise their children, communities, and cities. This was my work, my place, and I knew it."

Allie listened and was amazed by what

she was hearing. She had learned all about Cadillac in school and from her father, and now she was learning even more from Madame Cadillac herself.

Madame continued, "Fort Pontchartrain had been finished by the time we arrived. It was strong, made of oak, three **fathoms** (eighteen feet) high and walls thirty fathoms (180 feet) long. There were streets like Ste. Anne, St. Louis, and St. Joachim already laid out and rough-hewn cabins built of white oak with roofs of grass and branches. The houses were close together for protection. A powder magazine was also built to store supplies and gunpowder.

"Antoine invited many Indian nations to join us here and live in peace. He offered gifts of mirrors, bolts of cloth, thread, combs, black and green beads, porcelain and *eau-de-vie* (water of life), or what is called brandy.

"We were joined by bands of Huron and Odawa. Some Potawatomi and Miami people also came, and later, even some Iroquois. They called my husband *mon pére* (my father) and he called them *mes enfants* (my children). He loved these people and wished to live in peace with them. He wanted our people to marry together, to respect each other.

"If everyone could read and write, my dear Antoine believed it would help us understand one another and live in peace. He also made plans for a hospital. Nothing was more urgent for gaining respect of the Indians, he said, than helping them in time of illness. You see, many illnesses came to them from us and *l'Anglais*. Smallpox and fevers struck down the Indian people, who had never before known of such illnesses.

"And the Indians came often from distant places, such as Fort de Buade, where

Antoine was once commander."

"Where?" questioned Allie.

"Michilimackinac, another strait. . . ."

"Oh, up by the bridge." Allie remembered visiting a reconstructed fort by the Mackinac Bridge.

"Bridge? I know of no bridge." Madame Cadillac waved her hand and dismissed Allie's involvment in the conversation. "How that angered the Black Robes, the **Jesuits**. Even the building of a church, Ste. Anne, did not change their minds about my husband."

"They were mad because the Indians liked your husband?" questioned Allie.

"*Non*, my child. It was Antoine's gifts of *eau-de-vie* that angered the priests. They wanted no brandy to be used in the fur trade.

"And the jealousy. Ah, it raged as well. The traders at the other straits—what is the bridge you say—how they hated my great husband. His success at *le Détroit* would steal their trade, so they believed. They worked against him, Antoine Cadillac, a great man—a great man who is now forgotten."

"I don't understand how you can say that," said Allie. "My father said there are people from all over the world who live in this city. Isn't that what your husband wanted? And I know people can read and write because there is a great big library here and this museum, too. I know people learn from this museum."

Madame stared at Allie and said haughtily, "Yes, all this may be true, but do they know of my family and my husband's? Do they even know his name?"

"Yes! People know his name. There is even a car named after him," argued Allie in an indignant tone.

"*Oui*, that is true, but only because I stood beside the man that created this horseless carriage, Henry Leland, and whispered the name of my husband in his ear over and over. There were many whom I whispered the name of Cadillac to, but they did not listen. It was only this man, Leland, who could hear. And because he could hear, I was able to help him and his friend Henry Ford make Detroit an important place to make this carriage and many like it."

"You helped to make Detroit an automotive capital?" Allie began to question the claims of the woman with whom she seemed to be captive.

The woman looked away from Allie and lowered her head. "It was only this man that would listen to my voice. All the others, the others did what they could to destroy the good name of my husband and family. Especially Nain Rouge."

"Nain Rouge? I thought your husband's enemies were the priests and other traders. How did this gnome thing get involved?"

Madame paused for a moment. Tears came to her eyes and Allie could see her hand was trembling as she touched her pale cheek, deep in thought.

"Antoine had told me he believed there was an evil shadow that followed him around *le Détroit*. He said it watched him through the windows at night, or from behind trees as he walked outside of the fort. Then one night we discovered it was true.

"Antoine and I were strolling in the light of a full moon outside the **palisade**. It was beautiful along *le Détroit Riviére* (the Detroit River). He held my hand gently and we talked and were happy together. Soon a mist began to creep up from *la rivière*, and we decided it was time to return to the fort.

"As we followed the trail to the fort,

we thought we heard someone approach along the water in the mist. At first we thought it was a voyageur, arriving late to trade. But the trees suddenly began to shake, twigs snapped, and a cold rustling wind stirred all around us.

"Antoine stopped. He knew I was afraid and slipped his arm around my waist and pulled me close.

"Just then an owl who sat perched in a tree high above us swooped down, fluttering its wings in our faces. The rushing sound it made and the shadow of its great body passing in front of the full moon was frightening.

"Then the sound of the shaking trees grew and the mist became thick around us. 'Nain Rouge,' my husband whispered. It was a name that I had forgotten.

"My husband slowly drew his sword, and the drawing of the metal from its case sent shivers up my spine. In a loud voice he demanded the fiend show himself. Finally, out of the mist appeared a creature the size of a child. But when we looked closely we could see this was not a child at all!

"Its eyes seemed to glow and there were two small horns upon his forehead. He was dressed in a ragged cloak of crimson, and his hands were gnarled with sharp pointy nails. I cried out in terror as his chilling laugh filled the air and he reached out to touch me.

"Antoine pulled me back and stepped up to the creature who laughed wickedly again, showing his yellow fangs. Then, in an instant he disappeared into the mist leaving behind a stinking smell of sulfur."

Madame twisted her hanky in her hands as she remembered the incident. Goosebumps ran up and down Allie's arms and across her shoulders. Could this all be true? she wondered.

"The creature did not leave us for long. No sooner had he disappeared than he re-appeared behind us, circling around like a wolf.

"I will never forget how it looked and how it reached out again, this time touch-ing the fabric of my dress.

"To protect me my dear husband slashed the night air with his sword. The wicked thing disappeared again into the night mist, and his fiendish laughter faded away along *le riviére*. But on the ground in front of us, he left behind his ragged, stinking cloak of crimson.

"Antoine was so angered he slashed at the cloak over and over, pinning it to the earth and crying out for the creature to leave *le Détroit* and never return.

"Quickly we ran to the fort. Antoine ordered the gates closed. Then we ran to our home and barred the doors and windows.

"Even today I remember the look on Antoine's face. He was pale and frightened and his hands shook as they held mine. 'I fear I have brought tragedy upon us,' he cried. 'Do you not remember? Remember the warning of Mére Minique and the name Nain Rouge?'

"Slowly, like a book opening in the light of a candle, I began to remember."

7

CHAPTER

The Warning

Allie watched Madame as she took her hanky and gently dabbed the tears from her eyes.

"Yes, I remembered. I remembered a warning told to my husband a year earlier at a banquet in Quebec given in his honor by the governor of New France, **Louis de Callières**. It was something that I had tried hard to forget."

"What was the warning?" asked Allie. "Who was Mére Minique?"

Madame continued. "The warning was given the evening before my husband was to leave for *le Détroit*, and the memory I tried to forget now burns in my head like the blazing candles that filled the banquet hall that dark night."

Allie swallowed hard as she looked into the eyes of Madame Cadillac and listened to her every word.

"You see," the French woman continued, "many great men and their wives gathered there that evening to honor my husband for his courage and intelligence, because on the next morning, he would depart from Quebec on his journey to found a new city for the honor and majesty of France.

"After a sumptuous meal, stories were told about my husband's many brave deeds. Then there was merriment to be had. A woman by the name *Mére Minique, La Sorciére* (Mother Minique, The Sorcerer) was present to tell the fortune of the guests.

"On Mére Minique's shoulder sat a large, black cat that was said to whisper fortunes in the old woman's ear.

"Many of the men and women had their

fortunes told that night, but I warned my husband it was not a good idea to seek the council of one with a black cat upon her shoulder.

"My husband laughed at me, making fun of my silly ways. You see, I was a daughter of New France, from Quebec, and not as sophisticated as my husband, whose home was France and who had visited Paris and the great King Louis many times.

"I chose not to have my fortune told by this woman. But my husband was caught up in the fun of those around him. He playfully scratched the ear of the black cat that purred upon the woman's shoulder. Suddenly the cat reached out with its sharp claws and swatted at his hand, drawing blood. My husband only laughed at the creature.

"Antoine insisted Mére Minique read his fortune and stretched out his hand to her. I

remember it as if it were yesterday. Her eyes glowed and grew wide with horror and she looked away. '*Non, non,*' she said under her breath. I heard her say those words in fear.

"She released my husband's hand and from under her cloak brought out a silver bowl. She shined it with her skirts until it glistened and reflected the bright flames of the candles that surrounded us. Then she pulled a **vial** from the pocket of her skirt, removed its stopper, and poured a thick, clear liquid into the bowl. Replacing the stopper she put the vial back into her pocket.

"Again she lifted Antoine's hand and held it in her thin, gnarled fingers. This time she did not look at the lines in his hand, but peered into the silver bowl, watching the reflection of the candlelight upon the liquid.

"She breathed deeply and slowly and

closed her eyes. The black cat upon her shoulder arched its back, its long fur standing straight up. Then it hissed and growled in a low deep tone at my husband.

"Antoine laughed as the cat jumped down and ran away, hiding under the old woman's skirts.

"Mére Minique began to sway, still holding my husband's hand and the silver bowl of liquid. A low deep cry came from her parted lips, and soon it became a chant that she sang as she rolled her head from side to side.

"I reached for my husband's arm to draw him away, but he would have nothing to do with it. He laughed at my fear, while hushing me so that I would not disturb *la sorciére*. Soon tears fell upon the old woman's leathery cheeks, and she slowly opened her eyes as if staring into an invisible world. Then she turned and peered directly into my husband's eyes and shook her head in sadness.

"In a crackly voice she said '*Sieur*, soon you will travel on a dangerous voyage. You will be *pére* (father) to a great city filled with many people.'

"My husband shouted, '*Oui! Oui! Trés bien!* (Yes! Yes! Very good!) That is reason to celebrate, not for sadness. Is there more?' he asked.

"*La sorciére* said, '*Oui, sieur*, there is more. You will have conflicts with the Black Robes, *les Jésuites*. You will have conflicts with the fur traders. The natives will turn against you, and there will be much sadness. *L'Anglais* will claim your city, and you will die in the country of your birth.'

"Antoine was angered by the woman's words and insisted on knowing more. I pleaded with him, '*Non, Non mon ami. . . .*'

"He looked at the woman and asked,

'*Mes enfants*, they will inherit from my ambition, will they not?'

"The woman shook her head sadly. 'Beware of the Nain Rouge. Should you offend this being, there will be nothing for your children and your name will be forgotten in the city you will build in the wilderness.'

"My poor husband pulled his hand back from the woman and grew silent. The woman emptied the thick liquid from her silver bowl into a goblet and quickly drank it down, wiping her mouth with the back of her hand.

"Wiping the bowl again with her skirts, she tucked it away under her cloak. Her eyes glistened as she slowly stood and picked the black cat up from where it hid under her skirts. She stroked the fur of the cat, and sparks popped in the air between her fingers and its fur.

"Silently she walked through the party.

Everyone drew away from her while her cat hissed and swatted at the crowd. As she opened the door of the hall, a great gust of cold wind filled the room and extinguished many candles. Then she disappeared into the night.

"One by one people silently left my husband's side. Our host, Governor General Callières, laughed at the silliness of the old woman and tried to lift his guests' spirits. But everyone began to leave, fearing the fate of Antoine de la Mothe Cadillac and his family.

"Early the next morning I bade my husband *adieu* (goodbye), as he set off with his men and our son on their way to the wilderness.

"I was relieved to finally get word, weeks later, that he and our son had landed safely, and the **pickets** of the fort were soon to be complete.

"Months later, because of my husband's letter and my preparations to follow him, I had forgotten the silliness of that evening. I forgot the words of the sorceress. I forgot the name of Nain Rouge. I forgot, until I was forced to remember, that which I did not want to. And now offended, Nain Rouge was with us."

Allie scarcely blinked her eyes as she listened to the story. How could that fortune-teller know? she wondered. And how old could that red gnome be anyway? He couldn't live forever, could he?

Madame reached out her pale hand and touched Allie's. "It is a sad story, no?"

"Yes. It is sad. What happened after that?"

Madame sniffed and gently wiped her nose. "After that there were many times the Nain Rouge came after my husband and the people of the fort.

"Late at night the guards would hear a knocking on the gates of Fort Pontchartrain. Permission was sought from my husband, in the middle of the night, to open the gates.

"My husband would dress and go out into the cold night air and look over the palisade before the gate could be opened. Seeing nothing, he ordered the gates open.

"Once the gates were opened the mocking laughter of the Nain Rouge would be heard over the howling of the wolves and the moaning of the wind.

"Many times within the fort, the same thing would happen. A knock would come to the door of the soldier's **barracks** or to our home, or even worse, on the door of the priest's home. When the door was answered in the dead of night, no one was there. But there was always the sound of the strange mocking laughter.

"The Nain Rouge played many wicked pranks to scare the soldiers and workmen away from this place," continued Madame Cadillac.

"My husband said he once saw the creature walk through a sizzling fire at the fort's guard station. The guards had been frightened away by fiendish laughter and by a strange mist which rose from *le rivière* and crept slowly towards the fort.

"My husband was sent for immediately, but by the time he arrived the cowardly guards had hidden themselves behind the church of Ste. Anne. My husband alone witnessed the little creature dressed in crimson do **pirouettes** over the blazing fire. He danced without being burned and laughed his mocking laugh as my husband tried to chase him away."

"That's really weird," said Allie. "Why would anyone want to dance on fire?"

"This was just the way Nain Rouge worked to strike fear in the hearts of my husband's men so they would betray him.

"Over the months, whenever a hardship came to the fort the imp's laughter would fill the air and scare the people. When a terrible storm destroyed the roof of a house or lightning struck and burned a wood pile—whenever anything bad happened—Nain Rouge was blamed. The hardship of the people was the delight of that evil one."

"What a jerk," commented Allie.

"Once when a barn mysteriously burned to the ground, some saw Nain Rouge there. They said he picked a warm place to sit and watch the fire—right on the roof of the burning barn!

"We hoped it would be the end of Nain Rouge, but we learned better as he appeared over and over and laughed his horrible laugh, striking fear into the hearts of all the good people at *le Détroit*.

"At night all were fearful of the mist that came up from *le rivière*. Many said the mist was the coat of Nain Rouge, to replace the one my husband had foolishly destroyed.

"Many who arrived at the fort after the gates were closed, whether they were soldiers, traders, voyageurs, or fishermen, were afraid to approach the fort if they saw the mist. They knew Nain Rouge was waiting for them.

"It was said he would first walk slowly behind them, crackling the leaves they had crackled and snapping the twigs they had snapped. When the men became fearful and started to run, they would see the form of the Nain Rouge running at their sides and laughing at their fear, as if the creature were their very own shadows. He would chase the men until they reached the fort, shouting to the fort guards to open the gates. When the gates were opened, the men would fall into the fort, exhausted and crazed with fear.

"If they were fishermen, their fish would be lost to the beast of the woods. If they were hunters, the meat of the deer or bear would be lost to the crazed and starved wolves that fought and growled and howled outside the gates.

"Other times, the Nain Rouge would run around the palisade carrying a long wooden stick. As he ran, he dragged the stick along the wooden walls, making a wild noise. He would run around and around the great fort, just to frighten us all.

"One day in a lightning storm, a bolt of fire came out of the sky and struck the flag-pole that held our beloved lily of *la belle France*, the **fleur-de-lys**, (the lily of beautiful France: the flag). It burned the banner and the pole.

"And it was not long after this, in the fall of 1703, that a great fire broke out in the fort. It burned our church, the beautiful Ste. Anne, to the ground and then headed directly towards the store of gunpowder as if directed by the evil hand of Nain Rouge.

"Then the people of the fort knew the Nain Rouge would run them from their homes and the land they loved, and they began to leave."

8

Adieu le Détroit

Allie couldn't believe that the kid in the red tennis shoes could really do all those awful things. Where is he now? wondered Allie. He's with Shoo, she thought, frightened by her own answer.

"Whenever Nain Rouge appeared," continued Madame Cadillac, "destruction and fear were not far behind.

"Fights began to break out at the fort between the men. My husband even began to be afraid of Alphonse de Tonty, his second in command and husband of my best friend, Marie-Anne. Antoine thought Tonty and his men were forming against him to take away our city.

"Soon Antoine's enemies filed false

charges against him and sought to have him removed from his position here at *le Détroit*. He was ordered to return to Quebec to defend himself before the court.

"Was he arrested?" asked Allie.

"He was not, but detained in the city, keeping him away from his beloved *le Détroit* for nearly two years.

"While he was away the Indians began to fight. The Miami and Odawa caused much bloodshed. Afraid and alone with my children, I was allowed to return to Quebec to be with Antoine.

"Thankfully, there were those in France who believed my husband was a good man. They were powerful, more powerful than Nain Rouge. They sent letters from France to defend him and gave him even more power here at *le Détroit*.

"When we returned from Quebec, it angered Nain Rouge and my husband's enemies even more.

"Antoine soon had Tonty removed from the post. That left me without my friend, Marie-Anne. It was a lonely time for me then, as it is now.

"Life became difficult after that, but my husband was determined to see our settlement grow. But before his plans could be set, his patron **Frontenac** mysteriously turned against him as well.

"It was shortly after this period that an inspector was sent from Quebec to view the fort, which had fallen into ill repair while we were away. The inspector gave such a bad report, it was as if his pen was guided by the very hand of Nain Rouge.

"Antoine was heartbroken to think his friend Frontenac and the king had now turned against him. Soon an order arrived. I will never forget that date, November 3, 1710. My husband was told to proceed immediately to Louisiana to become the new governor of that place. It was disguised as an honor, but of course, it was not. Antoine was being forced to leave all he had worked for here in *le Détroit*, to leave his dreams behind and to be forgotten.

"The few families that were left at the fort fled to Quebec and Montreal. They knew if Antoine was no longer here to keep the Indian nations at peace, there would be more danger.

"They said that as they paddled up the river leaving their homes behind, they heard the mocking laughter of Nain Rouge bidding them *adieu*.

"Soon after Antoine was made governor of Louisiana we were sent to France, never to return to our beloved *le Détroit* again. Antoine was brokenhearted—broken by the evil of the offended Nain Rouge."

"All this because your husband slashed

his stinky cloak?" asked Allie.

"*Oui*," said Madame as she shook her head. "We lost everything. Antoine tried to claim our properties in *le Détroit* but discovered the land we held was greatly reduced. What remained was sold for only a fraction of what it was worth and what was due to us. My husband died in 1730, only eight years after he sold this land in the place of his dreams. He died in his homeland of France, far away from the place he had built.

"It was Nain Rouge who took it all away. That is why I have given my eternity to make my husband's name remembered."

"But his name is remembered. Why don't you believe me?" questioned Allie. "Your husband's name isn't forgotten. Everyone, or just about everyone, knows the name of Cadillac," insisted Allie. "It's true.

"My father has always said that knowing history and its stories will make the past live forever," said Allie. "We go to school and learn all about people like your husband. And we have libraries and museums, bookstores and computers that help us remember our past."

Madame listened to her words. "If this is true, then Nain Rouge has failed and can be destroyed. I hope the one you call your brother remembers the past and knows the name of Cadillac. That wicked creature is using you and your brother to prove my dear husband is forgotten.

"I am afraid if your brother does not know the name of Cadillac, you too may be trapped here forever."

"What? How can he do that?" asked Allie. Just then Shoo appeared at the top of the stairs with their mother, followed by the impish Nain Rouge in red tennis shoes.

"Mom!" called Allie, greatly relieved to

see her. "Mom, I'm right here. Can't you see me?"

Mrs. Spywell, looking worried, quickly passed by her daughter and Madame Cadillac as if they did not exist and entered the dark doorway into the exhibit hall. Shoo followed, walking right through Allie's invisible form.

"Hey!" shouted Allie.

"I don't know where she went, Mom!" Allie could hear Shoo's voice. He sounded concerned. "I thought she went upstairs with you."

As Nain Rouge followed them, he sneered at Allie. He tipped his red baseball cap to her, revealing two small horns that grew out of his forehead.

Allie reached out trying to break through the glowing bubble of blue haze that held her invisible and silent from her family. Nain Rouge laughed at her attempt.

Soon Mrs. Spywell reappeared in the doorway. "Shoo, I want you to wait here in case Allie comes back. And don't go off with your friend, okay? Keep an eye out for her. I'm getting worried." Shoo looked over at the boy in the red cap and nodded.

"I'll watch for her. She'll probably be down here any second," said Shoo.

The Nain Rouge smiled, turned to Allie, and whispered, "Perhaps she is here now."

"You mean old thing! You'd better leave me alone," cried Allie. "Mom! Shoo!" But neither her mother nor brother could see or hear her.

"I am going to check the bathroom and then go find your father. Maybe she is with him in the car exhibit."

"Mom," Allie shouted again, just inches from her ear. "You have to hear me! Mom!"

Allie's mother paused on the landing and

looked behind her. "What was that? Shoo, did you hear something?" Mrs. Spywell crossed her arms and shivered. "It's cold right here for some reason."

Shoo shook his head. He hadn't heard anything. Nain Rouge raised his eyebrows and wiggled them at Allie.

Slowly Allie's mother climbed the stairs. Then she paused again and looked back at the landing.

"You cannot save yourself, but your brother can," whispered Nain Rouge in Allie's ear. "I heard you tell Madame that people remember her husband, whom I despise," hissed the red gnome in Allie's face. His smelly breath reminded Allie of a bucket of worms. "You say that I have failed to banish his memory from time? I see in your eyes, you believe what you say," he continued. "So I will ask you this—does your brother remember?"

Allie paused for a moment, thinking about all the times she had teased Shoo and tried to make him feel like he wasn't smart. She knew Shoo really was smart, but would he remember Cadillac?

"I'll ask you again. Do you believe your brother will remember?" snarled Nain Rouge.

9

Prove It!

"Yes!" shouted Allie. "Shoo, will remember!" She wished she were as certain as she sounded.

"Then you must find a way to make him prove it. That is, unless you want to keep this woman company for an eternity.

"You see, Madame here has spent her eternity trying to make the memory of her husband live in this place." Nain Rouge pointed his stubby finger towards Madame Cadillac. "You have told her the name of her husband is not forgotten, that I have not done what I said I would do. But Madame is the one who has failed. I say the memory of her husband is already forgotten. Unless your brother speaks the name of this woman's husband," he said as he glanced across at Madame Cadillac, "it will prove that her husband has been forgotten. Unless your brother speaks his name, you will stay here with her forever."

Suddenly, a clear loud voice came over the intercom of the museum. "The museum will be closing in fifteen minutes. Please make your way to the front exit. Thank you."

"Perfect," snarled the little gnome. "Your brother has until the museum closes to say the name. This will prove my enemy is forgotten."

"You can't make us do anything," said Allie. "You have no power over me or my brother."

"Oh, we will see," hissed the Nain Rouge, "just how much power I have. You would be amazed how easy it is to lead someone away from a name, a story, or a dream."

Just then Shoo poked his head out the doorway and looked at the Nain Rouge. "Hey, who are you talking to? It sounded like my sister out here. Did you see her?"

"Well, not unless she is invisible," responded Nain Rouge with a laugh.

Shoo grinned, "Yeah, I guess you're right, unless she was invisible." Shoo looked up the dim staircase to the top.

"I wish she would show up. She didn't even see the Streets of Old Detroit exhibit. She would have really liked it. She's a brain, you know, she's always thinking. Don't tell her I said so, but she's the smartest girl I know. She's always talking about history and books and stuff like that with our parents."

Allie, surprised by her brother's words, smiled and stared meaningfully at Nain Rouge. We'll show that little creep we remember the past, thought Allie.

"Don't worry, your sister is probably right here. You will see her soon enough."

Shoo turned and looked in surprise at his friend in the red cap. "Why do you say that? Did you see her?" asked Shoo.

Nain Rouge ignored Shoo and tried to change the subject. "Have you seen the entire exhibit? There are some really neat things here, like an old dentist's office with sharp drills and ugly looking pliers that were used to pull people's teeth without even numbing them. Can you imagine how much that would hurt?" Nain Rouge asked with a cruel smile.

"That would really be bad. I am glad our dentists know more today," said Shoo.

"There are also long pointy hatpins, stuck in a cushion in the window of the hat shop, and an old blacksmith shop with hammers and a forge. Come on, you've got to come see the rest. It's really cool," insisted

Nain Rouge as he put a coaxing hand on Shoo's shoulder.

"Allie, come! We must find a way to keep Nain Rouge from making your brother forget," urged Madame. "We will work together. You will help me." Madame stood, placing her invisible form in front of Shoo, no longer afraid of Nain Rouge.

"Cadillac! Cadillac!" she repeated her husband's name over and over.

"What's that?" asked Shoo. "Do you hear something?"

Allie and Madame stood in their transparent form and loudly called the name of Cadillac.

"I think I hear Allie." Shoo turned looking up the stairway.

"It's nothing. Come on, you will miss the fire department."

"No, you go on. I'm going to stay here. I keep thinking I hear Allie's voice. Allie?"

called Shoo. His voice echoed up the stairs. "Allie?" he repeated.

Allie cupped her hands and tried to encircle Shoo's ears, but her hands kept passing right through her brother. "Shoo," she shouted with Madame. "Say the name Cadillac! Cadillac!"

"Allie?" called Shoo again as Allie and her ghostly partner tried their best to be heard.

Nain Rouge sneered at their efforts. Allie reached out for him and grabbed his cold, leathery hand. "How dare you, you creep!" she screamed in his face. "Leave my brother alone!"

"Allie, no!" cried Madame. "Do not touch him!"

Nain Rouge waved his finger in the air and suddenly Madame's voice disappeared.

"You be silent now! I dare you, Madame, to challenge Nain Rouge! Look where it got your husband."

Allie turned and saw Madame Cadillac moving her mouth, calling the name of Cadillac. But her voice had now become as silent to Allie as her body was invisible to others.

Allie turned toward Nain Rouge and marched right through Shoo, who continued looking up the stairs. Standing, half in and half out of her brother's body, she put her hands on her hips and leaned forward to face Nain Rouge.

Nain Rouge was laughing so hard he held his belly. Allie noticed that his fingers now looked gnarled and misshapen and he had long, sharp fingernails.

"Who do you think you are? You're not going to win, you horrible thing! My brother knows the name of Cadillac!" She shouted in Nain Rouge's face.

At the sound of the name Cadillac so

close to him, Nain Rouge threw back his head and let out a long, angry, wolf-like howl.

Shoo jumped nearly out of his skin as the silence of the stairwell was broken.

"Hey, what do you think you're doing? What's the matter with you?" demanded Shoo as he turned around and walked right through Allie to Nain Rouge. "You scared the bejeebers out of me. You sounded just like a wild dog or something."

"Oh, I'm sorry. I just like to hear the sound of that echo in the stairway, that's all. I like the sound of a wild wolf, don't you? Don't you think it would be neat to be a wolf or perhaps a werewolf?"

"No!" said Shoo. "I think that's really weird."

"Cadillac!"

"Shoo!" called Allie. "Shoo!" Shoo stopped and quickly turned facing his invisible sister, eyeball to eyeball, Allie's form passing right through her brother's body. "Shoo!" she called again.

"Did you hear that?" asked Shoo to his strange friend. "I keep thinking I hear Allie's voice calling to me, but when I listen, it's not there. I wish she would show her face. Maybe my mom found her in the bathroom. She was carsick earlier, so maybe she got sick again."

Allie watched as Madame Cadillac stood near the old trunk and mouthed the name of her husband over and over.

Allie again began repeating the name of

Cadillac to Shoo. "Come on, Shoo, this is no time to forget history. Come on, say the name of Cadillac. Cadillac! Cadillac!" Each time Allie spoke the name, Nain Rouge cast an icy stare at her right through Shoo.

"Hey, what's the matter with you?' asked Shoo. "Why do you keep looking at me so weird?"

Nain Rouge focused on Shoo, not knowing what to say. "Ah, ah, you know, I think you might be right. I think I hear a girl's voice calling, too."

"You do?" said Shoo eagerly.

"Yeah, I think it sounds like it is coming from the exhibit. You better go look. I'll wait here and watch, just in case your sister reappears." He grinned at Allie.

"Yeah, okay. You wait here,"said Shoo as he darted through the doorway into the exhibit, looking for his sister.

Nain Rouge quickly turned to Allie and

Madame and waved his ugly hands in Madame's direction. Her voice instantly returned. "You think the name of your husband lives?" asked Nain Rouge. "You are wrong and it will never live again." He curled his lips to reveal his yellow fangs at Madame.

"And you!" He blew his hot breath into Allie's face. "I will make you a promise," he snarled. "If the name of that vile man, this woman's husband, is not spoken. . ." he pointed to Madame Cadillac. "If it is not remembered and repeated by that human you call your brother before the closing of this museum, then you both will be lost and forgotten. You will disappear into the history of this city, never to be heard from again. You will be gone and no one will even remember you existed."

Allie couldn't believe it. This thing, this Nain Rouge was threatening her again!

123

"Who do you think you are? You're a weirdo!" shouted Allie.

Nain Rouge lifted his gnarled hand toward Allie. "Silence!"

"How dare y. . . ." Allie's voice froze in her throat. She could move her mouth, but her voice wasn't there.

"We will see who is stronger, me or the memory of my enemy," said Nain Rouge as he turned into the exhibit.

Allie tried over and over to call her brother's name, but her voice did not come. Madame reached for her. "My poor dear, see the games he plays. He is a bad one. We must believe, believe your brother remembers the name of my great husband."

Allie didn't know what to do. Her voice was gone, she was invisible, and if Shoo didn't say the name of Cadillac before the museum closed, they would be stuck here forever. Allie knew this was a nice museum, but forever was a long time.

Madame pulled her hanky from her lacy sleeve and handed it to Allie. But Allie was too angry for tears. Where did her mother go? Where was her father? she wondered. She knew they could make Shoo say the name of Cadillac.

Shoo soon reappeared in the doorway. "She's not down there. Hey, it's been really cool meeting you and everything, but I think I better go look for my parents."

"Why don't you stay here with me? Your parents will come to look for you," Nain Rouge smiled slyly.

"No really, it was cool meeting you and everything. And the exhibit was neat. It was really creepy and everything. I sure wish Allie would have had a chance to see it—and meet you, too. You would have liked her, but I have to go."

"What if your sister shows up? If she gets

locked in, maybe she will have to stay here forever."

"Yeah, right. You're really funny. She is probably up there with my parents gabbing like they always do."

"Perhaps she went outside and lost her way," suggested Nain Rouge.

"No, she's not stupid. She knows better than to leave the building. My parents would be really mad if she did that. Anyway, she likes history too much. She is just like my dad, always the last one to leave a museum."

"Last one to ever leave the museum," laughed Nain Rouge.

"What did you say?" questioned Shoo as he stared coldly at the impish boy who was beginning to irritate him.

"Oh nothing, I didn't say anything."

Allie gave Nain Rouge a dirty look.

Madame now stood beside Shoo and repeated the name of Cadillac over and over in his ear.

Shoo stood silent for a moment and listened.

"Weird, I keep thinking I hear something. It must be my imagination. Well, I've got to go. I know I will probably find my mother in the bookstore with Allie. Boy, did Allie miss all the excitement!"

Madame kept repeating her husband's name over and over as silent Allie waved her invisible hands in front of Shoo's face.

"You know, it is really chilly here in the stairway. They need to do something about the air conditioning. It's weird."

Nain Rouge stood beside Shoo and stood half in and half out of Madame. "Yeah, you are right," he said glaring at Allie, who kept waving her arms and fanning the air.

"I think I'll go find my dad first. He is supposed to be up in the old car exhibit.

Allie might even be up there with him. He wanted to see those cars in the worst way. He even said he wanted to be a race car driver, that is, if he wasn't an archaeologist."

Allie waved her hands over and over, but she just wasn't getting through to her brother. Madame called to Shoo, but it was no use. A loud voice came over the intercom again. "The museum will be closing in five minutes. Please make your way to the front exit. Thank you."

"Yeah, I better go," said Shoo as he turned and started up the stairway. "I wonder if Dad found that old car or at least a picture of the one he was looking for. You know, the one named after that French guy Cadillac."

The instant Shoo said the name of Cadillac, Nain Rouge froze in his place. Allie watched as Shoo continued up the stairs and through the doorway, looking for

Allie and his parents.

"He said the name!" said Madame with pride. "He said the name of my husband! You are right. Your brother is smart, *trés magnific* (very magnificent)! Antoine's name has not been forgotten."

Instantly Allie's voice returned. She reached out to Madame and they hugged. "Hoorah for Shoo!" cried Allie.

"Look!" pointed Madame Cadillac as the form of Nain Rouge began to change. No longer did he look like a boy. His skin grew red and leathery, his ears pointy, and his fangs came down over his lips.

Soon the creature began to shiver and shake, throwing its arms around and knocking its red cap off. Pointy toenails shot though the ends of his red tennis shoes.

Allie and Madame Cadillac moved away from the creature as he began to spin faster and faster. Soon he was just a blur to their eyes. Suddenly, tiny red blobs filled the air, sparked into flames, and then disappeared. It was if Nain Rouge had become one of the fireworks on the Fourth of July.

Allie looked down at her hands. She began to glow from the inside, and a cold icy wind swirled around both her and Madame.

In the distance a faint, low voice could be heard, "Marie Thérèse? Marie Thérèse?" Madame looked at Allie in surprise as the voice grew louder.

"Marie-Thérèse. . .Marie-Thérèse. . ."

Madame's eyes grew wide in delight. "It is the voice of my husband," she said. "A voice I remember from so long ago. One that I have never forgotten."

"Marie-Thérèse," the voice called again, this time very loud and clear.

"I must go to him," she said as the wind whirled around them. "He is waiting." Madame looked deeply into Allie's eyes. "You are right, my child, people do remember. They are taught to remember. Nain Rouge has failed and my job is now finished," said Madame Cadillac with a smile. "Remember, always remember the past." With that the image of Madame began to fade as she floated upward towards the top of the stairs. There in the doorway stood the form of a man dressed in fancy clothes with a **tricorn** hat upon his head and a large feather stuck into its gold braid.

Madame's form paused. She looked back at Allie and waved her lilac scented hanky, "*Merci, mon amie* (Thank you, my friend)." The man at the top of the stairs removed the hat from his head and bowed deeply to Allie, smiling in appreciation. Then he reached out to his wife, who placed her pale, delicate hand in his as they both gently faded away.

"Allie!" shrieked a voice making her al-

most jump out of her skin. "Where have you been?" Shoo was standing on the very spot where Madame Cadillac and her husband had disappeared.

"Where have you been?" he repeated.

"I. . .I. . . ." Allie didn't know what to say. Just then her parents appeared behind Shoo.

"Allie, get up here!" snapped her mother. "Where have you been, young lady? The museum is getting ready to close. I thought they were going to lock you in."

"We have been looking high and low for you!" added her father.

Allie climbed to the top of the stairs. "I've been right here. I've been hoping you'd see me."

"What?" questioned Shoo.

Allie's mother put her arm around her daughter and gave her a hug. "I'm sorry I snapped at you. I was just so worried. We didn't see you down here. You must have been afraid," she added, "not being able to find us."

Allie nodded her head as she cast a glance back towards the trunk on the landing.

"I knew you should have joined me in the car exhibit," added Mr. Spywell. "Detroit really is the Automobile Capital of the World."

"Allie, you missed it! The Streets of Old Detroit is really cool. And there was this kid with a red cap—did you see him? He knew all about this place. And guess what?" continued Shoo. "He liked to howl like a wolf, too."

Mr. and Mrs. Spywell looked at Shoo and frowned. "A wolf?" they asked in unison.

"Yeah, he was kind of strange. But you know what was stranger? He said he didn't even like history. He said he thought it wasn't worth remembering."

"Is that so?" questioned Mr. Spywell lifting his eyebrows. "And what do you think, Shoo?"

"I think there is lots more history out there than what we know, and I think it's pretty neat," said Shoo as he smiled up at his father.

"So did you see him?" Shoo turned to Allie and asked.

"Yes," said Allie as she thought about all that had just happened. "I saw him. I saw him as he left," she said, greatly relieved to be back with her family. She smiled and then laughed out loud as she watched Shoo skip, hop, and twist his way to the museum exit. "Cadillac, Cadillac, Cadillac," she heard him chanting.

Glossary

acclaim. To be welcomed with great honor.

Algonquian. One of many languages spoken by Native Americans. Also a person who speaks this language.

archaeologist. One who scientifically studies past human lives and civilizations.

Automobile Capital of the World. At one time a nickname for Detroit because of the booming automobile industry that was started there.

barracks. A large building or group of buildings for soldiers to live in.

Belle Isle. Known as Wah-na-be-zee or White Swan Island to the pre-1700 Americans and Hog Island to the French and British, renamed Belle Isle in 1845. Declared public domain in 1701 by Cadillac. Purchased in 1768 by George McDougall for eight barrels of rum, three rolls of tobacco, six pounds of vermilion, and a belt of wampum. Purchased by City of Detroit in 1879 and designated a public park.

birch bark canoe. A canoe made from the bark of a birch tree.

botanic garden. Where plants and trees are grown for scientific study.

Cadillac, Sieur Antoine de la Mothe. (1658-1730) A French colonial administrator who was granted a large tract of land to start a settlement which became Detroit.

Callières, Louis de. (1646-1703) Governor of Montreal and governor of Canada after Frontenac.

cloak. A loose, sleeveless outer garment, often called a cape.

coat of arms. A design on a shield which is an emblem for a family or city.

commandant. Officer in charge of a fort or military installation.

cryptozoologist. A scientist who studies questionable or unusual species.

Detroit Grand Prix. World class car race held in Michigan. While at Belle Isle the race was held on a temporary 2.36 mile road course.

Detroit Public Library. Currently located across the street from the Detroit Historical Museum. This library was created as a result of an 1842 ruling by the Michigan Supreme Court declaring penal fines were to be credited to a library fund that would found and finance a public library.

Detroit River. River that connects Lake St. Clair with Lake Erie and forms part of the U.S.-Canada border.

Father Dollier. A priest and the first Frenchman to claim the area of Detroit in the name of France.

fathom. A measure of six feet used in stating the depth of water.

fleur-de-lys. The emblem of the royal family in France. It resembles three flower petals bound together.

Ford, Henry. (1863-1947) Industrialist, best known for pioneering the automobile industry in Detroit, Michigan.

Fort Pontchartrain. A fort founded by Cadillac in 1701 and built in what is now the city of Detroit.

Fort Wayne. Built in 1840, this is the only river fort standing from Detroit's 300-year history.

Frontenac, Comte de Palluau et de. Louis de Buade. (1620-1698) French colonial governor of New France (the French possessions in North America) from 1672 to 1682 and from 1689 to 1698.

frontier. The edge of settled territories.

fur trade. The business of buying and selling the skins of animals. The fur trade in North America was one of the primary reasons for European settlement.

General Motors. An automobile producer located in Detroit, Michigan.

geologist. A scientist who studies the earth's crust and strata.

gnome. This imaginary creature is described in folkore as a small, shriveled man who lives underground and guards the earth's treasures.

Great Manitou. The all-powerful creator in Native American beliefs.

Huron Indians. Native American tribe that lives/lived in the Great Lakes area. At the time of Cadillac their numbers had been greatly reduced by smallpox and battles with the Iroquois.

Jesuit. A member of the Society of Jesus Roman Catholic religious order. Jesuit missionaries traveled to remote areas seeking to convert the native people.

Lake St. Clair. Located between Detroit and Canada. Although it is not one of the five Great Lakes, Lake St. Clair lies between lakes Huron and Erie and is connected to them via rivers.

La Salle, Sieur de, René-Robert Caveliere. (1643-1687) French explorer who traveled the Great Lakes and navigated the length of the Mississippi River, claiming the Louisiana region for France.

league. A measure of distance typically about three miles.

Leland, Henry. (1843-1932) Detroit car manufacturer. Founded Leland & Faulconer Mfg. Co. (1890), Cadillac Motor

Car Co. (1904), and Lincoln Motor Co.

Louis XIV. (1638-1715) King of France from 1643-1715. He was known as the Sun King.

magnetic charges. Power produced by charged particles in a magnetic field.

mannequin. A dummy for displaying clothes.

Marquette, Jacques. (1637-1675) Born in France and trained as a Jesuit priest. In 1673 Marquette accompanied Louis Jolliet and five others on a journey of discovery to the Mississippi River.

Mississippi Valley. The valley that follows the flow of the Mississippi River from Minnesota to the Gulf of Mexico.

Montreal. Canada's largest city at the time and chief point of entry.

moor. To secure a boat or vessel to a fixed object.

Motown. Nickname for the city of Detroit. It is derived from the nickname "Motor City."

Neptune. Mythological god of the sea.

Neutral Indians. Also known as the Neutral Nation because they took no stand for or against the Huron or Iroquois. The Neutrals lived on the northern shore of Lake Erie and were eventually destroyed by the Iroquois.

Odawa (Ottawa) Indians. Native American tribe that lives/lived in the Great Lakes area.

Ojibwa (Chippewa) Indians. Native American tribe that lives/lived in the Great Lakes area.

oracle. A person or thing that was known to give wise advice.

palisade. A fence of stakes set closely together in the ground to defend an enclosure.

pickets. Posts or stakes used to make a fence or enclosure.

pirouette. A whirling about on one foot or on the toes.

Pontiac's Rebellion. Chief Pontiac led hundreds of warriors against the British at Fort Detroit. The siege lasted 153 days.

Quebec. French-Canadian city on the bank of the St. Lawrence River below Montreal, located on the site of an old Indian town.

Rouge River. River which empties into the Detroit River near Belle Isle and Grosse Ile.

shrine. Any place or object which is revered for its history or association.

strait. A narrow body of water linking two larger bodies of water.

superstition. An idea or belief not based on knowledge or reason, usually giving great significance to some object or event.

transformation. To make a great change in appearance or character.

tricorn. Having three horns or projections.

vial. A small bottle for holding liquids.

voyageurs. Canoemen, mostly French-Canadian, who transported furs throughout the Great Lakes region and beyond, from the early seventeenth century until the mid-nineteenth century. They were the backbone of the fur trade.

Biographical Information

Antoine de la Mothe Cadillac

Born March 5, 1658, in St. Nicholas-de-la-Grave, Gascony, France. He spent his life serving as a French military officer, explorer, and administrator. In 1697 he presented to the French king, Louis XIV, a plan for a permanent settlement in New France that was designed to protect the French interests in the North American fur trade. With the king's approval, Cadillac became the founder of Fort Pontchartrain, Detroit, in 1701. He also served as governor of French Louisiana from 1713 until 1716. He was buried on October 16, 1730, in France.

Marie-Thérèse Guyon Cadillac

Born April 9, 1671, in Beauport, New France (near Quebec). She was the daughter of a successful merchant. She married Antoine Cadillac in June of 1687, in Beauport.

She had 13 children, five of which did not survive childhood. Marie-Thérèse departed her home in Canada on September 10, 1701, to join her husband in the new settlement of Detroit. She arrived at her destination in the spring of 1702. Marie-Thérèse moved with her husband to many different parts of North America and eventually to France, where she died in June of 1746, in France.

Cadillac and le Détroit

1658: March 5, Antoine Laumet (later to adopt the name Antoine de la Mothe Cadillac) is born in St. Nicholas-de-la-Grave, France.

1667: Antoine Laumet enters military duty. He is appointed a cadet in the regiment of Dampierre-Lorraine and soon becomes lieutenant in the regiment of Clairambault, Paris.

1669: Louis Jolliet travels the Detroit River on his way east.

1670: Father Dollier claims the area for France.

1671: Simon Francois, Sieur de St. Lusson, claims the Great Lakes region for Louis XIV.

1679: The *Griffin*, the first sailing vessel on the Great Lakes is built by La Salle, and sails through the straits of Detroit.

1680: La Salle marches across southern Michigan to the Detroit River.

1683: Antoine sails to New France and settles in Port Royal, Acadia (Annapolis Royal, Nova Scotia).

1686: Plans are made to establish a fort at le Détroit.

1687: June, Cadillac marries Marie-Thérèse Guyon of Beauport, Quebec.

1688: Cadillac acquires a grant of land in Acadia (Nova Scotia).

1689: Cadillac travels to France to provide information of the Atlantic seaboard. He returns to New France.
Cadillac befriends Governor Frontenac and is appointed lieutenant in colonial troops.
Cadillac is assigned aboard a ship to patrol the shores of Acadia to protect it from the British.

1692: Cadillac in France for a meeting with Count de Pontchartrain concerning the defense of New France and the fur trade.
Cadillac works with mapmaker Franquelin charting the coast of New England.

1694: Cadillac is appointed Commandant of Fort du Buade (Michilimackinac, St.

Ignace).

1696: Cadillac and the Jesuit mission of St. Ignace at odds concerning the Indians and fur trade of the Straits. Cadillac asks to be relieved.

May 1, King Louis XIV orders withdrawal from western post.

1697: Cadillac joins his family in Quebec.

1698: Governor Frontenac dies and is replaced by Louis de Callières.

1699: Cadillac goes to France to petition Count Ponchatrain to establish a fort at le Détroit to protect the fur trade and land holdings from the English. Cadillac is granted 15 arpents of land to establish a post at le Détroit.

1701: May 12, Cadillac arrives in Montreal to buy supplies for his expedition.

June 4-5, Cadillac leaves Montreal with 25 canoes carrying 50 soldiers and 50 workers/settlers. He brings his 9-year-old son, Antoine, along. Cadillac's second in command is Pierre Alphonse de Tonty.

July 23, Cadillac arrives on Grosse Ile.

July 24, Cadillac leaves Grosse Ile and returns upstream to the narrowest point, le Détroit. He begins to build Fort Pontchartrain.

1702: Spring, Madame Cadillac arrives with son Jacques and de Tonty's wife.

1703: Fire at Fort Pontchartrain.

1704: Madame Cadillac gives birth to the first white child born in Detroit, Marie-Thérèse.

1705: September 5, Company of the Colony turns over trading rights in Detroit to Cadillac.

1706: While Cadillac is in Quebec his temporary commander, de Bourgmont, involves the French in fighting between the Odawa and Miami Indians.
Cadillac has de Tonty, who has been opposing him, removed from the post.

1707: November, Pontchartrain sends an investigator to the fort.

1709: Detroit troops are ordered to return to Montreal and abandon Detroit.

1710: November 3, Cadillac is ordered to take over the governorship of Louisiana and leave Detroit immediately.

1711: November, Cadillac returns to France and leaves family in Detroit.

1712: Mass Indian uprising at Detroit.

1713: Cadillac and family leave for Louisiana.

1715: Cadillac follows the Mississippi to Illinois country while looking for silver, copper, iron, and lead.

1716: Cadillac recalled from his position in Louisiana.

1717: Cadillac returns to France. He and his son are arrested for speaking against the government.

1718: Cadillac released from prison and tries to claim his Detroit property but fails to do so.

1722: Cadillac sells his remaining property in Detroit and purchases an appointment as governor and mayor of a town in France.

1724: Cadillac is removed from office.

1730: October 6, Antoine de la Mothe Cadillac dies, age 72, France.

1746: June, Marie -Thérèse Cadillac dies, age 75, France.

Other Books by Janie Lynn Panagopolous

Great Lakes Adventures in History & Mystery

The Runes of Isle Royale
Calling the Griffin

Dream-Quest Adventures

Traders in Time
Journey Back to Lumberjack Camp
Erie Trail West
North to Iron Country
Train to Midnight

An Adventure in History

Little Ship Under Full Sail